IT'S FUN TO LEARN ABOUT
SIZES

Claire Llewellyn
Consultant: Dr Naima Browne

ARMADILLO

NOTES

This book introduces children to the concept of size. Lively pictures and stimulating activities encourage them to understand and compare the differences between sizes.

Learning the basics

This book shows children that size is one of the ways in which we group things. Matching, sorting and classifying are important concepts. They lie behind the mathematics covered in the first year of school.

Reading together

You can help your child by reading aloud the words that accompany the pictures. Go through the book at your child's pace, looking at a couple of topics at a time. Allow plenty of time to talk about the ideas before moving on to talk about others. This way, reading times are enjoyable.

Talking it through

Help your child's understanding by encouraging them to talk about the pictures and relate what they see to their own experiences. This will help your child to develop self-confidence and make the ideas meaningful.

Learning by doing

Encourage your child to try the activities. They can help to extend and develop skills further. Try to make everyday activities an adventure in learning – tidying a wardrobe or going to the supermarket offer plenty of opportunities to talk about size.

Checking your child's understanding

Check your child's understanding of size by asking useful questions about everyday activities. For example, when you are laying the table for a meal you could ask – Which spoons are the biggest? Which glasses are the same size? Always remember to praise your child.

CONTENTS

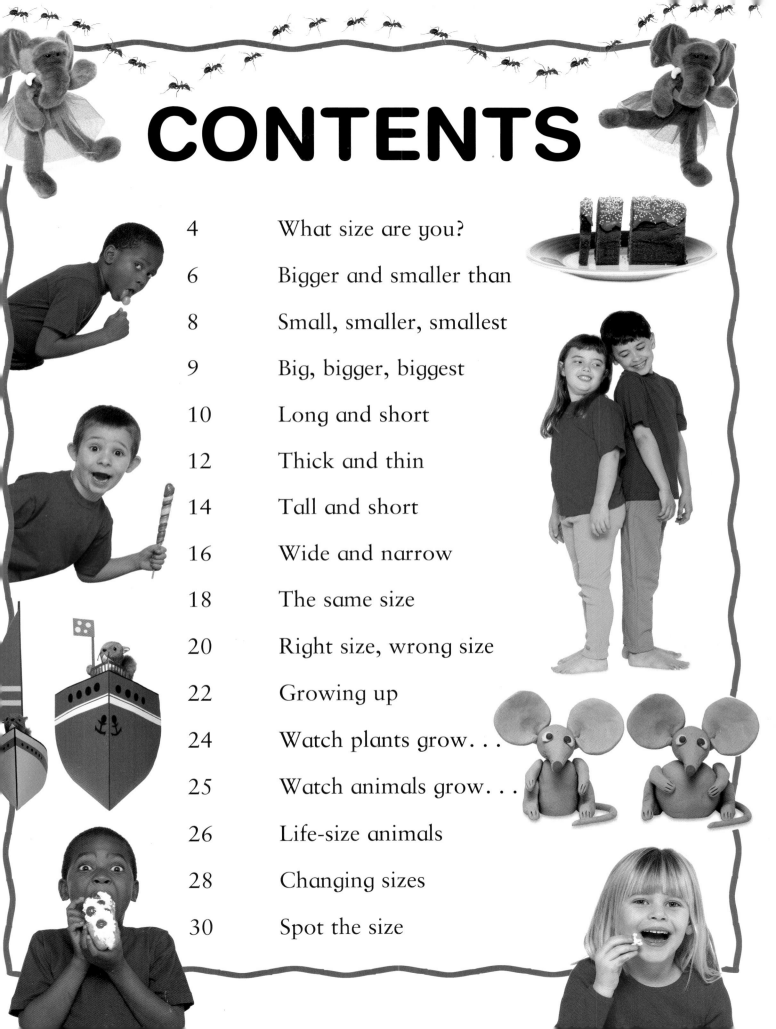

What size are you?

Tall, short, little, big – all of us have the same sort of shape, but we come in many different sizes.

I can stretch myself out wide.

I can hold myself in until I'm as thin as a pin.

Who is taller? You, o your friend Take off yo shoes, stan back-to-bac and see who is taller.

Massive Ted is much bigger than me.

Little Ted is smaller than me.

4

My legs don't stretch very far yet.

My legs are longer.

I have the longest legs of all three.

When you do a forward roll . . .

you go from tall . . .

to a small, tight ball.

Stretch up tall . . .　　bend your knees . . .　　crouch right down . . .　　and tuck in your head.

Is your hair . . .

. . . short, . . .

. . . long, . . .

. . . or in-between?

Bigger and smaller than

Look around you each day to spot people, places and things that are bigger or smaller than each other.

An Afghan hound is much bigger than . . .

a Yorkshire terrier.

enormous present

smaller present

big rabbit ears

smaller cat's ears

My small lollipop will soon be gone.

My bigger lollipop will last all day long.

The small fish is after the big shark's tail. Uh-oh!

My big shopping bag is too heavy to lift.

My small handbag is light to carry.

Would you prefer a big bunch of flowers . . .

or a pretty little posy?

RUN!

You are much smaller than the dragon and his great big flames of fire.

These beads are small. I can hold dozens of them in my hands.

These beads are smaller. I can hold hundreds of them in my hands.

Have you heard the story of Pinocchio?

His nose grew bigger . . .

and bigger . . .

every time he told a lie.

Small, smaller, smallest

We sort small things in order of size: small, smaller and the smallest of them all.

small ladybug

smaller ladybug

smallest ladybug

Small peas always seem to taste the sweetest.

Which frog has the smallest parachute?

Three mice sailing across the salty sea.

Spotted fish swimming, one, two, three.
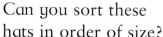

Try this!

Make three-size cookies

1. Buy some ready-made cookie dough. Find three cutters of different sizes.

2. Roll the dough flat with a rolling pin.

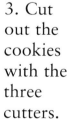

3. Cut out the cookies with the three cutters.

4. Bake in the oven until they are lovely and golden brown.

Can you sort these hats in order of size?

Big, bigger, biggest

Spot the **biggest** ballerina . . .

Long and short

Can you sort long things from short things?
Look at the objects on this page, then try
to find others at home.

short-tailed lizard

long-tailed lizard

Here is a short line of elephants waiting for a bus.

A super heroine
can fly off quickly
in a short cape.

A king walks
slowly in a
long cloak.

The bus has not arrived yet and the short line has become a long one.

Short socks cover
my ankles.

Long socks almost
reach my knees.

Yum! Yum!

If you had a choice of long, slurpy
spaghetti strands or short pasta bows,
which would you want to eat?

Try this! Make a slinky snake

1. Get nine paper cups and paint them.

2. Take a cup for the head. Stick an eye on it.

3. Using a pencil, carefully make a hole in the bottom of the cup.

4. Thread string through the hole and tie a knot.

5. Join the cups together with paper fasteners.

Pull your slinky snake along.

Most cats have long tails, but the Manx cat has a short, stubby one.

long neck

If my neck was as long as a giraffe's, I could see high above the trees.

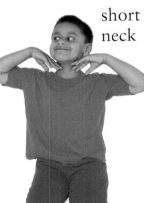

short neck

Did you know?

The giraffe's neck is longer than any other animal's.

Will you grow a moustache when you are older?

Will your hair be long or short?

Thick and thin

Would you choose the thick or thin things on this page? Is one better than the other?

Two monkeys are swinging on ropes.

Hey!

Look at me!

Which rope do you think will break?

Help yourself to a piece of cake. Which slice would you like?

Did you know?

Polar bears have thick fur coats to keep them warm in the cold.

The wizard's thick book of magic is full of weird and wonderful spells!

The teddy bears' book is thinner. A quick read!

How shall I wear my hair . . .

in two thick plaits . . .

or in lots of thin plaits?

Which spiders have the thickest legs?

A thick sweater warms you up on cold days.

A thin T-shirt keeps you cool on hot days.

This frog and squirrel are painting.

Are their paintings the same?

A thick rubber ring will help you to float in water.

Can you spin a hula-hoop around your waist?

Would you rather munch on a very thick sandwich or a very thin one?

Try this!

Thick and thin sandwiches

1. Ask an adult to cut four slices of bread – two thick and two thin. Butter them.

2. Ask for two slices of cheese – one thick and one thin.

3. Now ask for four slices of cucumber – two thick and two thin.

4. Make one very thick and one very thin sandwich.

thick sandwich   thin sandwich

Tall and short

There are tall and short things all around us.
Which ones are taller or shorter than you?

Are you taller than your teddy bear?

Which of these towers has more beakers?

We need a taller ladder to rescue Chicken from the tower. This short ladder will not reach to the top.

A dessert is a delicious treat. Which one would you choose to eat?

Try this!

Who wears a hat?

1. Think of two people who wear hats. Draw them on a piece of paper.

2. Now think about their hats. Are they tall or short? Draw them on the picture.

3. Finish your picture with felt-tipped pens or crayons.

Pull out the sides of a bendy mirror and it will make you look short. Push in on the sides and you will look taller.

Look at these two teddy bear towers. Which one is taller?

Can you spot any differences between these two hats?

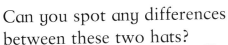

a tall blade of grass

a short one

15

Wide and narrow

Spotting whether things are wide or narrow is a way of seeing how much space they take up.

wide sunglasses   narrow sunglasses

wide tie   narrow tie

Stretching out to walk through a wide gap.

Squeezing through a narrow gap.

A mouse hole is wide enough for a tiny mouse but too narrow for a fat cat!

Which is the wide boat and which is the narrower boat?

wide blue sea

16

A big car needs four wide wheels.

A skinny bike only needs two narrow ones.

Lots of narrow bangles will easily fit on your arm.

How many wide bangles will fit on your arm?

Two elephants wobble along a narrow tightrope. Are they going to make it safely across?

Spiders scuttle along a wide plank.

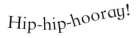

Some ribbons are wide and silky. Others are narrow and fine.

Would you choose to wear . . .

narrow, clingy leggings . . .

or wide, baggy trousers (pants)?

Hip-hip-hooray!

For an eye-popping finale . . . stretch your arms out as wide as you can.

The same size

Two socks, two shoes, two gloves – when two things are the same size, we say that they make a pair.

A clown's sh

Ted is balancing on a pair of skis.

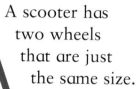

Two shoes in the same size make a pair.

Now he can slide down the snowy mountain slope.

A scooter has two wheels that are just the same size.

Make sure that your roller skates are the same size!

Some musical instruments come in pairs.

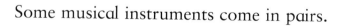

Crassh!

Crassh!

You need two cymbals to make a loud noise.

Shake your maracas gently for a soft sound or hard for a loud one.

Tsshh

Tsshh

Whose shoes?

A pair of shoes that tinkle and curl. Who can they belong to?

Glittery party shoes

A perfect fit! The prince has finally found his princess.

Two cold hands need two woolly gloves.

Do you think these gloves will fit?

Look at yourself closely in the mirror.

You have two eyes and two ears just the same size.

What other parts of your body are the same size?

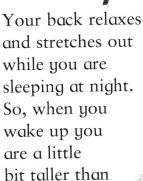

Did you know?

Your back relaxes and stretches out while you are sleeping at night. So, when you wake up you are a little bit taller than you were the day before.

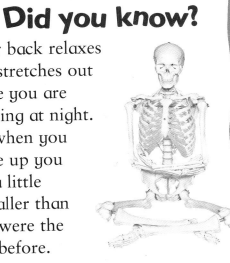

19

Right size, wrong size

It's important to have some things just the right size. You cannot ride a bike that is much too big, or wear shoes that are too small.

Are these children wearing the right-sized clothes?

This chair is the right size.

Oops! This one isn't.

Try this!

Make a paper doll

1. Draw a paper doll. It can be anything you want – an animal or a girl or a boy.

2. Lay see-through paper over the drawing. Draw some clothes for the doll.

3. Cut out the clothes and stick them on the doll. Do they fit?

Can you eat a cream cake in just one bite?

A small mouthful of cheese is almost right.

A piece of popcorn is just the right size.

hese shoes
re the
rong size
or me . . .

. . . but these
shoes fit
perfectly.

Did you know?

You need to be measured
to know which
clothes and
shoes are
the right
size for you.

Two teddy bears
are going for a ride.

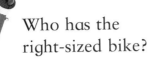

Who has the
right-sized bike?

Are these suitcases
the right size?

too big

too
small

The wrong-sized toothbrush.

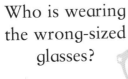

Who is wearing
the wrong-sized
glasses?

The right-sized toothbrush.

growing UP

Our body changes as we get older. We grow taller and wider and we need bigger and bigger things.

A one-year-old baby can crawl.

A three-year-old toddler can walk and run.

An eight-year-old child can do things f-a-s-t!

Babies grow out of their clothes very quickly.

Toddlers learn how to dress themselves.

A bigger child needs bigger clothes.

A baby wears slippers to keep its feet warm.

A toddler's shoes slip on and off easily.

How old were you when you first tied your shoelaces?

Some babies are carried in safety chairs like this.

How old do you think the owner of this tricycle is?

Stabilizers will help you balance when you learn to ride a bike.

A 13-year-old teenager
is tall and strong.

At 25, you may have
stopped growing!

Try this!

See how you grow

1. Hang a big
piece of paper on
the wall. Stand in
front of it and ask
a friend to draw
around you.

2. When you
step away from
the paper, the
drawing will
show the shape
of your body.

3. Do the same
thing one month
later. Ask your
friend to draw
around you in
a different pen.

Whose shirt is this?

Do you like to wear
fashionable clothes?

4. Take a ruler
and measure the
difference between
the two body
shapes. Have
you grown?

Sneakers are easy and
comfortable to walk in.

High-heeled shoes are
harder to walk in.

When you are older,
you can ride on the road.

Only adults
are allowed
to ride a
motorbike.

23

Watch plants grOW...

Plants and animals are living things, too. Like people, they start life small but, as long as they have plenty of food, they soon begin to grow.

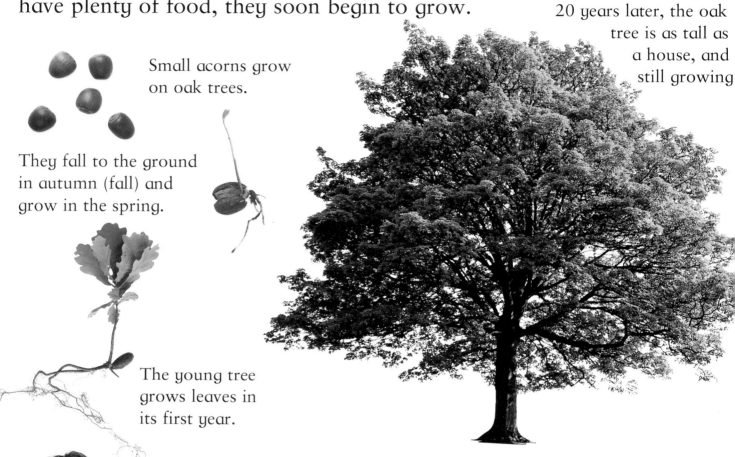

Small acorns grow on oak trees.

They fall to the ground in autumn (fall) and grow in the spring.

The young tree grows leaves in its first year.

20 years later, the oak tree is as tall as a house, and still growing

Try this! Grow some sprouts

1. Soak some mung beans in water overnight. Drain them and leave in a covered jar.

2. After two days, the beans will start to sprout. Sprinkle them on top of a delicious salad.

Watch animals grOW...

Baby animals grow more quickly than humans. In just a couple of months, they may be ten times bigger than when they were born.

When kittens are born, their mother licks them clean.

Even after one week a kitten's eyes are still tightly closed.

At three weeks, the kitten has started to move around. But it is still not very strong.

Nine weeks old, and the kitten is almost ready for its first trip outside.

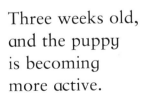

This puppy is three days old. It only sleeps and eats.

Three weeks old, and the puppy is becoming more active.

At five weeks, puppies begin to be curious about the world around them.

After eight weeks the puppies are ready to go to a new home.

This baby owl is resting after hatching out of its shell.

A group of two-week-old owlets wait for a meal.

Four weeks old, and the owlets are moving around their nest.

After twelve weeks, an owlet loses its fluffy feathers and is growing fast.

Life-size animals

All the animals on this page are shown life-size. Are they bigger or smaller than your hand?

Are we the smallest creatures on this page?

Quack!
Quack!

This duckling hatched just two days ago!

Soon this puss-moth caterpillar will turn into a gorgeous butterfly.

Are these baby mice smaller than your thumb?

Squeak!
Squeak

This baby tortoise takes bigger steps every day.

Purrrrr!
Purrrrr!

This small kitten would look enormous to a tiny mouse!

Ladybirds crawl through the garden, eating bugs even smaller than them!

Watch out! A python is coming this way – and its body is as long as a bus!

Snails have eyes at the end of their feelers. See how long the feelers are.

Tortoiseshell butterflies stretch out their wings to soak up the sun's rays.

A tarantula's legs are longer than a snail.

A guinea pig's whiskers are wider than its face.

Changing siZes

How can you change the size of something?
By stretching or shrinking it, or puffing it
up, or breaking it into bits!

You can build a big
castle with lots of
little bricks.

Break a big bar of chocolate
into little squares and share it
with your friends.

My T-shirt
is too small
for me now.
It must have
shrunk in
the wash.

Yum! Yum!   Oh dear!

I am hungry.   Now I am full.

You need a
lot of puff
to blow up
a balloon.

Puff, puff!
It is
getting
bigger.

Puff, puff!
Now it
is even
bigger.

My skirt has an elastic waist. It fits me perfectly. Or it can stretch and stretch to make room for two.

A small amount of cake mixture becomes a big cake after it is cooked.

Can you put all the pieces of a jigsaw puzzle together?

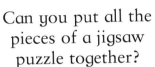

Pop!

Now it is the same size as when I started.

Try this!

Make a picture puzzle

1. Draw a picture on a piece of thin card. Fill it in brightly.

2. On the back, draw four or five wiggly lines across the card.

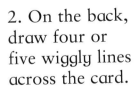

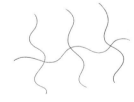

3. Cut the card into pieces along the lines.

4. Ask a friend to put the puzzle pieces back together again.

Spot the size

Take it in turns to throw the die and move your button around the board. When you land on a square, look for the answers on the page. You have ten seconds to do this. If you can't, miss a turn. If you can, you have another go. The first one to finish is the winner.

You will need 2 buttons or markers, a timer and a die.

START

1 Find another ladybug of the same size.

2 Just how big can his nose grow? Find an even bigger one.

3 Find me with my blown-up balloon.

4 I've got thin legs. Find the spider with thicker legs.

5 Find the smallest frog.

6 Find a lizard with a long tail.

7 Find a tall dessert.

8 Find a bigger ted.

9 Find a wide bangle.

10 Find someone with a short moustache.

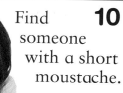

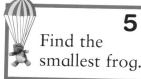

13

Find a shorter tower.

14
Find a longer blade of grass.

15
I was thinner before I ate that cheese. Where is the thinner me?

16
Find a narrower boat.

11
Find a thicker sandwich.

12
Find the same-sized boot.

17
Find an older kitten.

FINISH

21
Find someone who is stretching out wide.

20
These shoes are too big – find me a pair that will fit properly.

19
Find the wrong-sized toothbrush.

18
Whoops! Elephant has sat on the wrong chair. Find the right-sized chair for him.

This edition is published by Armadillo,
an imprint of Anness Publishing Ltd,
108 Great Russell Street,
London WC1B 3NA;
info@anness.com

www.annesspublishing.com; twitter: @Anness_Books

Anness Publishing has a new picture agency outlet
for images for publishing, promotions or advertising.
Please visit our website www.practicalpictures.com
for more information.

A CIP catalogue record for this book
is available from the British Library.

Publisher: Joanna Lorenz
Senior Editor: Felicity Forster
Educational Consultant: Dr Naima Browne,
    Department of Education, University of London
Photography: John Freeman
Stylist: Melanie Williams
Designer: Tessa Barwick
Production Controller: Ben Worley

PUBLISHER'S NOTE
Although the advice and information in this book are
believed to be accurate and true at the time of going to
press, neither the authors nor the publisher can accept any
legal responsibility or liability for any errors or omissions
that may have been made nor for any inaccuracies nor for
any loss, harm or injury that comes about from following
instructions or advice in this book.

Manufacturer: Anness Publishing Ltd,
108 Great Russell Street, London WC1B 3NA, England
For Product Tracking go to: www.annesspublishing.com/tracking
Batch: 7557-23943-1127

ACKNOWLEDGEMENTS
The publisher would like to thank the following children for
appearing in this book: Africa, Alice, Andrew, April, Callum,
Caroline, Daisy, Faye, Grace, Holly, Jackson, James, Jasmine,
Jason, Jerome, Joseph, Josh, Kadeem, Lateef, Lucie, Lucy, Luke,
Madison, Milo, Miriam, Otis, Philip, Rebekah, Rhys, Rosa,
Ruben, Safari, Sumaya, Tom, Zaafir, Zamour.

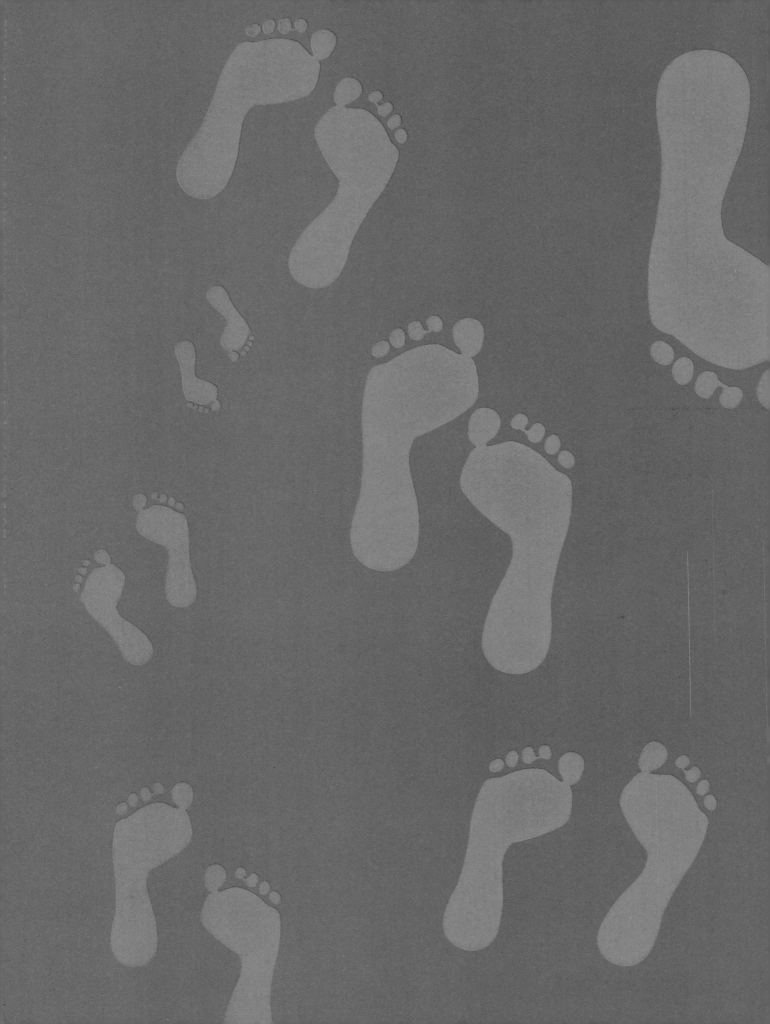